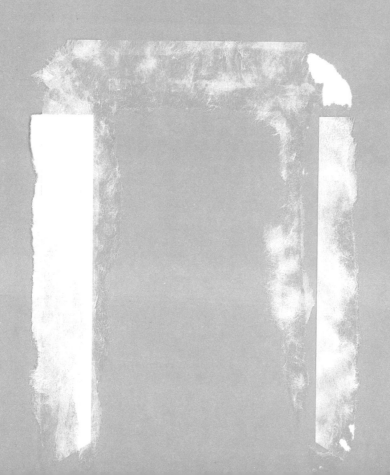

# MR. BIDDLE AND THE BIRDS

# Mr. Biddle and the Birds

by LONZO ANDERSON

Illustrated by ADRIENNE ADAMS

This book is from the:
santa clara county library district

CHARLES • NEW YORK

TO LAURA GREEN

A Voyage to Cacklogallinia, *an 18th century political satire by Samuel Brunt, has as its frontispiece a drawing similar to the "flying boat" in this story. We used it in the end papers of* Bag of Smoke, *a book about the beginning of human flight, in balloons. It was such a delightful picture that it kept picking at us and finally pushed us into doing the present story about Mr. Biddle and the birds.*

Mr. Biddle lay in his hammock. He watched his four bird friends fly in. They were coming to have lunch with him, as usual. How big they were, how strong, how beautiful in the air.

"I am thinking of flying with you," Mr. Biddle shouted. "It must be wonderful!"

Crown was the leader of the birds. He landed on the table first. Then, thud-thud-thud, came the other three, Adso, Badso, and Charlie. The birds started gobbling the food.

Mr. Biddle came to the table. He was very excited.

"Don't you hear me?" he asked. "I am thinking of ways to fly with you." He took a piece of paper and a feather-pen. He drew a picture.

"Look at this sketch," he said, "and see how you like it. Come, you can *eat* any time, for heaven's sake!"

The birds looked.

"A little boat on poles," Crown said.

"A chair-in-the-air," Adso said.

"A cradle-in-the-ladle, a porch-in-the-snorch," Badso said.

Charlie giggled. "A house-in-the-blouse, a kitchen-in-the-snitchen . . ."

"Oh, shut up!" Crown shouted. "Mr. Biddle, it's a good idea, the little boat, with us carrying it!"

"Well, then," Mr. Biddle said happily, "let's make it!"
He did not even stop to eat. He started pulling out of
the barn all of the things he would need.

The birds tried to help with the work at first, but they only got in the way. Adso brought some pieces of string, in case Mr. Biddle should wish to make a nest.

"Hmmm," Mr. Biddle said. "Maybe you'd better let me build this myself. There will be plenty for you to do later."

Soon the birds were chasing each other all around the sky, quarreling and screaming like hoodlums.

"I wonder," Mr. Biddle said to himself. "Am I wasting my time? They can't think of anything but play, fight, and eat-eat-eat."

Still, he kept on building the air-boat. He added a canvas cover, in case of rain. When the job was done, he called in the birds.

"It's just great!" Crown said.

"We can have fun with this," Adso said.

"Good," Mr. Biddle said, pleased as pudding. "But we shall have to have some corsets made for you before we can work it."

"Corsets? What are they?"

"They are to connect you to the poles. Remember the sketch I made? You hook the corsets on, and fly away, with me in the flying boat. Come to the corset-maker; you will see what I mean."

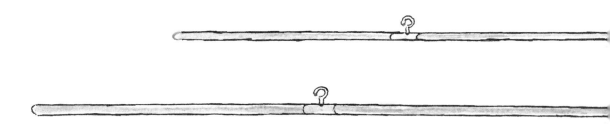

Off to the village they all went.
They felt silly at the corset-maker's shop.

Crown said, "I'm not sure I like this—but go ahead."

When the corsets were fitted, the birds could not wait.
Crown shouted, "Here we go!" and led the way.
"No, no!" Mr. Biddle cried. "We're not ready yet!"
He started running.
"We have to *think* about it, and *plan ahead!*"

By the time he reached home, the birds had hooked
themselves to the poles in any old way. *Flap-flap* they worked
their powerful wings.

Away went the flying boat! Mr. Biddle came gasping
for breath and made a dive into it, just in time.

"Hooray!" Adso screamed. "It's off the ground!"

Mr. Biddle hung on. His heart went *bang-bang-bang*.
The birds began to fight.

"Get out of my way!" Adso cried. Their wings were
getting all tangled up.

"*You* get out of *my* way!" Badso bawled. The flying
boat bounced and jounced and twisted.

"Where do you think you're going?" Crown shouted.
They were trying to fly in different directions!

"Where do you think *you're* going?" Charlie cried.

Mr. Biddle was tumbling out. He barely managed to get back inside.

Birds screamed. Such confusion!

The flying boat was falling, hurtling toward the earth.
*"Oh! Oh! Oh!"*
Down, down, wings all wrong.

*Crash!*
　　　Deep into a forest.
　　Then:
　　　　Silence.

One by one the birds pulled themselves free. Mr. Biddle crawled out.

"Is everyone all right?" he asked, worried. The birds just looked at him.

"Is anyone hurt?" Mr. Biddle asked again.

"A lot you care!" Badso shouted angrily. The other birds made furious noises.

"You nearly killed us!"

"You wanted to fly, hi-dee-hi, through the sky!"

"Hitching up birds like horses! We're not meant for that!"

Mr. Biddle looked at them a minute.

"Forget it," he said. "Flying is no fun. Terrible disappointment!" He turned and walked away.

He went through the woods toward home, and never looked back.

The birds stared at each other for a while, too shocked to make a sound. Then they came to life.

"Flying is no fun! Did you hear that?"

"Why, flying is the only fun there is!"

"What have we done?"

"We didn't have to act that way."

"We can make this thing work the way he wanted."
"If we can fix it."
"Come on, let's try!"
"It doesn't look too bad."
They lifted the flying boat down onto level ground.
Then they did something they had never done before:
They worked—and worked—and worked.

Finally Adso said, "There. Good as new."

"All right," Crown said. "Places, everyone. Let's do it right this time. Don't hook on side by side. Leave room for the other fellow to work his wings. Like this—me in front on the left. Charlie, you a little behind me, on the right—and so on. Good. No fooling around, now. Remember, it's for Mr. Biddle. *Concentrate*!"

"Take-off!" Smooth as a breeze!
Up, up!

They were delighted with themselves.

They flew over Mr. Biddle's house and looked down. He was lying in his hammock.

"Look up, Mr. Biddle!" Adso cried, high in the sky.

"Ssh! He's asleep," Crown said. "Let's surprise him."

Down they went, slanting, sloping, sledding along the wind, down and down. Their great wings made whispers in the air.

As they were landing on Mr. Biddle's lawn, something went *squeak*.

"Ssshh! Ssshh!"

But Mr. Biddle woke up. He jumped out of his hammock.

"Surprise!" the birds shouted together.

Mr. Biddle rubbed his eyes.

"Hop in," Crown said. "Let's go for a spin around the sky."

Slowly Mr. Biddle climbed in and sat down. He looked dazed.

The birds took off, *whoosh-oosh-oosh*. High they climbed, up, up, and higher. The whole world lay below, a marvelous view.

Still the flying boat lifted, lifted, higher, lighter.

Mr. Biddle leaned out, and spread his arms, and smiled, and sighed.

"Ah!" he said. "It *is* wonderful. I *knew* it! Thank you, my good friends."